This Book Belongs To

_____

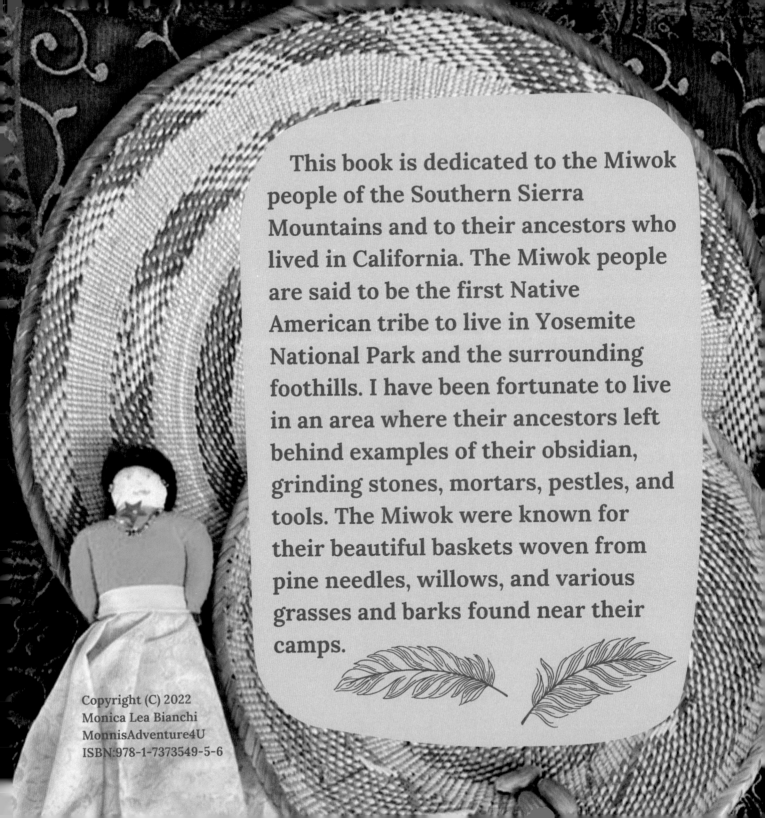

This book is dedicated to the Miwok people of the Southern Sierra Mountains and to their ancestors who lived in California. The Miwok people are said to be the first Native American tribe to live in Yosemite National Park and the surrounding foothills. I have been fortunate to live in an area where their ancestors left behind examples of their obsidian, grinding stones, mortars, pestles, and tools. The Miwok were known for their beautiful baskets woven from pine needles, willows, and various grasses and barks found near their camps.

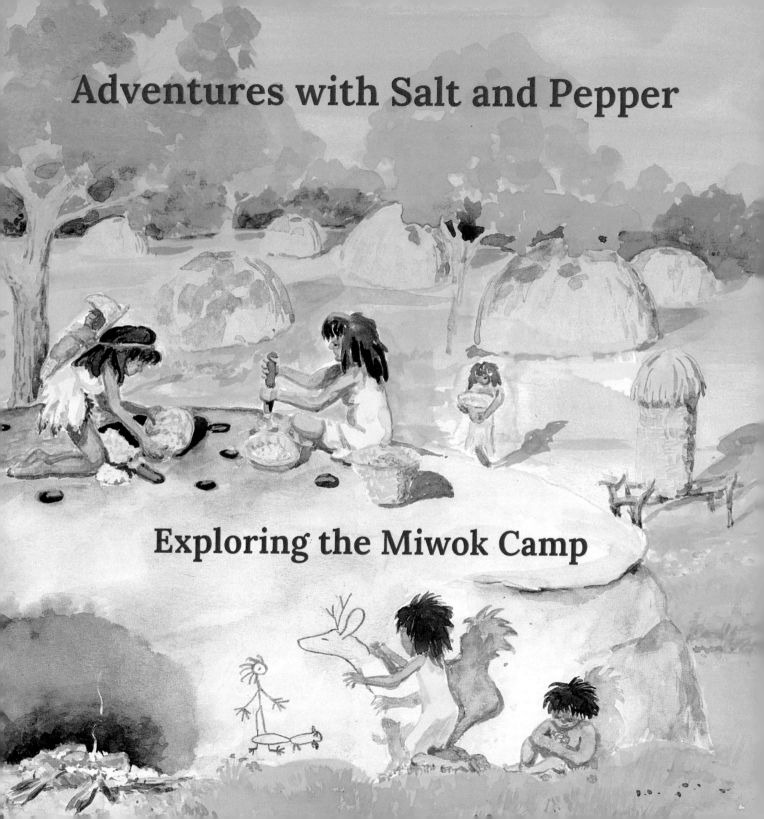

Adventures with Salt and Pepper

Exploring the Miwok Camp

Saturday is my favorite day of the week. On Saturday my mom makes waffles with syrup. I love to sit and watch cartoons with my little brother Rusty, but I really love to go on adventures with Salt and Pepper.

Today I'm so excited because I'm going on a special trip with Salt and Pepper. We are riding to the old Miwok Indian camp. It is far away, so I packed a big lunch. My favorite sack lunch is a couple peanut butter and jelly sandwiches. What's your favorite sack lunch?

I'm going to wear my favorite leather Indian vest that my grandma made for me for Halloween. I always wear my cowboy hat, so the sun doesn't burn my nose. This is the cool bow and arrow my grandpa made for me. The Miwok Indians hunted for animals with their bows and arrows.

When I was 6 years old, I found this cool arrowhead. It's shiny and black like glass. This rock is called obsidian. It was made inside of a volcano and then it blew out and the Miwok people found it. Someone made this sharp arrowhead by smashing it with rocks and bones.

Brutus, little Susie dog, and Bobbi the cat have to stay home. It's too far for them to walk and there are too many stickers in the tall grass. They look sad because they can't come.

Having a pet means you need to feed and water them every day. My rooster Pepper and his friends like to eat dried yellow corn and grain. Grain is the name for a mix of hard pieces of rice, oats, and barley. Salt likes to eat grain too, so, I'm taking a bag of grain for Salt and Pepper to eat for lunch.

Puffy clouds can sometimes bring rain. I brought my rain jacket to be safe. Today I'm going to put a Western saddle on Salt so I will have a comfortable seat and a place to tie my jacket and canteen.

See those big rocks and Oak trees way out in the field? That's where the Miwok camp used to be. I bet they made their home there because they had the creek and lots of acorns to eat. All sorts of animals live there too!

This tree has big round nuts; it's called a Buckeye. Buckeye nuts are poisonous so no animals or people can eat them. I guess somebody thought the brown nut looked like a daddy deer's eye, so they called it a buck eye. A buck is the name of a male deer. What's a female deer called?

Sometimes I get to see deer out in the field eating grass by the cattle. We must walk very carefully in this area because there are so many squirrel holes. Salt could trip in a hole and break his leg if we go too fast. Cattle can be dangerous, so we should stay away from them especially if they have horns!

What do you see Salt? When Salts' ears perk up that usually means he sees something. Look, over there by those bushes! I think I see some deer and a baby fawn. Fawns are the baby deer, and when they are young, they have spots on their back so they can be camouflaged in the weeds and bushes.

We're here! These holes are where the Miwok would grind their acorns into flour. It takes a long time to make a deep hole in a rock. The Miwok must have used these holes for many years to make them so deep. Oh no, a gray tree squirrel dropped an acorn on my back!

In the trees are gray tree squirrels. Their color is gray to match the tree bark. Why do you think the color of their fur is important? Have you ever seen a squirrel? What kind of a squirrel did you see?

See all the squirrels by those holes? Those are ground squirrels, and they live in holes underground. They are brown like the color of the dirt. They carry the acorns into their holes so they can eat them in the winter.

I found my first arrowhead around these squirrel holes. The squirrels loosen up the dirt and make the buried obsidian rock and arrowheads pop up. The best time to look for arrowheads is after a rain when they are shiny like glass. What's that near Pepper? It looks like a piece of shiny obsidian!

Way to go Pepper!
You found a carving or scraping tool! This is a
sharp obsidian rock that the Miwok people
may have used to cut things. What do you
think the Miwok people used it for?

This is the first time I found a crescent shaped piece of obsidian. I can't wait to show Mom!

I love collecting rocks and feathers and cool stuff that I find on my adventures. This feather in my hat looks like a wild turkey feather. I found it when Salt and I were at the creek last year.

What kind of things do you like to collect?

We are sitting on a giant grinding rock having our lunch. My house is down there! Salt loves his grain and Pepper wants to eat my sandwich.

My grandpa says that the Miwok liked this camp because there are a lot of acorns to eat; and because the creek is nearby to get water. It's important to have a camp by water so you always have something to drink. Talking about water makes me thirsty. Right now, the creek is dry, so I'll have to give Salt and Pepper fresh water from my canteen.

This area must have been the main Miwok camp. I drew those pictures on the rocks using charcoal from the old fire ring. I imagine that Miwok kids used to draw on these rocks while their parents were busy cracking acorns and making arrowheads.

The Miwok are a tribe of people that lived in California. Because the weather is usually warm, they made their homes out of branches and tree bark. They didn't live in a teepee like other tribes.

When I was six years old, I got to go camp with my grandma and grandpa way over there in Yosemite National Park. Yosemite (Yo-sem-i-tee) is a beautiful park where you can see giant waterfalls, and ginormous mountains made of pure rock. Oh no, I see lightning!

Yosemite is my favorite place to go because it has all sorts of trails to explore. The biggest trees in the world live there, the Giant Sequoias. In the summer the Miwok tribe would walk to Yosemite to hunt for deer.

Wow, those clouds are starting to get darker, and they are coming closer. I can smell rain in the air. It smells like wet dirt, so I know it will rain soon. The wind is getting stronger, and the tree leaves are starting to blow. I better get my stuff and go home before the rain comes.

Boy, I hope we get home before it starts to rain, it's getting very windy.
Oh no, my hat!

The squirrels are starting to go into their holes. I can see the cows in the pasture moving towards the trees and putting their backs to the wind. You can learn a lot by watching the animals.

Poor Pepper, are you OK?
This wind is very strong and I'm starting to
feel some rain drops on my back. Let me put
you in my jacket Pepper and then you'll be safe.

Look at all the leaves getting blown off the trees. This wind is so strong that those crows can barely fly.

Whoa Salt, we made it! Thank you, Salt, for taking us on another great adventure. Look out Pepper! This saddle is really heavy, and I don't want to squash you.

Hurry, Pepper! We need to get home before it gets dark. I'm sorry you have to walk, but I'm too tired and hungry. This wet gear is sure heavy, when it's all wet.

Oh Pepper, look at how wet you are! Here's some extra grain and corn for you since you were such a good boy today. Eat up Pepper, before the hens jump down and take your food!

Home at last! These steps are sure hard to climb when I'm all wet and carrying so much stuff. I sure hope we are having something good for dinner. I smell spaghetti!

Look what I found! It's a half-moon shaped obsidian rock! I bet it's a carving or scraping tool that the Miwok used! Isn't it neat? My mom always likes all the cool stuff I find except for live animals like snakes and mice!

I'm gonna put this scraping tool in my old Miwok basket so it will be safe with my arrowhead and all the other treasures that I've found. I feel so lucky that I live by a big ranch that is near the old Miwok camp.

Maybe during Spring vacation, my mom and dad will take us camping to Yosemite National Park. That would be so exciting! Wouldn't it be great if Salt and Pepper could go and maybe even my friend Molly? Where's a special place that you would like to go on an adventure?

Howdy!
I'm Monni, and this is my dog, Toby. This is my second book in the series "Adventures with Salt and Pepper". My books are meant to allow the reader to explore new places while meeting new animal friends, just as I did as a child. I hope you enjoy the adventures with us.

Monica Lea Bianchi

Hi, I am Molly, and this is the 13th published book that I have had the privilege of illustrating. My mother was a fine artist who encouraged my sisters and me to draw, paint and to sculpt as we grew up on a ranch in California. Later, I married a cowboy, and we raised our family on ranches in California and Oregon. One of the ranches was right in the middle of Miwok country; and we had old camps in some of our pastures, just like the one Monni found. It has been a joy to bring these characters to life.

Molly Pearce Combs

Made in the USA
Middletown, DE
08 December 2024

66305823R00024